Exchange Students

The last two girls climbed down from the bus and glanced around for their hostesses. One was wearing jeans and Mercury jogging shoes, exactly like mine.

When we got closer, we saw from her nametag that the girl in the jogging shoes was Kate's visitor, Darlene Kastner.

Darlene stared down at my feet in their Mercurys and her face lit up. "Am I staying with you?" she asked.

I shook my head. "No, Annette Hollis is." I was disappointed, because she looked like fun.

The last girl, who had to be Annette by process of elimination, was standing with her back to us. She didn't seem even a little curious about finding her hostess.

I sighed. I had a feeling it was going to be a very long week.

Look for these and other books
in the Sleepover Friends Series:

Lauren's Sleepover Exchange

Susan Saunders

AN
APPLE
PAPERBACK

SCHOLASTIC INC.
New York Toronto London Auckland Sydney

ISBN 0-590-41697-9

Copyright © 1989 by Daniel Weiss Associates, Inc. All rights reserved. Published by Scholastic Inc. APPLE PAPERBACKS is a registered trademark of Scholastic Inc. SLEEPOVER FRIENDS is a trademark of Scholastic Inc.

12 11 10 9 8 7 6 5 4 3 2 1   9/8 0 1 2 3 4/9

Printed in the U.S.A.   28

First Scholastic printing, February 1989

Chapter
1

"All right, class," Mrs. Mead said at the end of Social Studies one Friday afternoon. "If you'll put your books away and sit quietly, we'll have the drawing."

Kate Beekman, Stephanie Green, Patti Jenkins, and I — I'm Lauren Hunter — grinned at each other and crossed our fingers.

Mrs. Mead lifted the round clay pitcher she used for flowers off the top of her bookshelves. "As you know, nine fifth-graders will be coming from Walden Elementary School on Sunday to spend the week with us here in Riverhurst," she said, carrying the pitcher back to her desk. "Five girls and four boys."

Walden is upstate, about two hundred miles

from Riverhurst. It's a small farming town. Mrs. Mead, our teacher, is friends with Ms. Powell, a fifth-grade teacher at Walden Elementary. Between them, they had cooked up an exchange program: First, some of Ms. Powell's Walden fifth-graders would visit our class and learn about life here in Riverhurst. Later on, some of Mrs. Mead's fifth-graders would visit Walden.

Mrs. Mead sat down and picked up her pen. "I'm going to write the names of the Walden students on slips of paper," she explained. "More of you volunteered to have a visitor stay in your home — eight Riverhurst girls and six boys, to be exact — than we'll have visitors. So there'll be some blank slips in here, too."

Mrs. Mead finished writing, folded up some of the slips of paper, and dropped them into her pitcher. "If you draw a slip with a name on it, that person will stay with you." If you drew a blank slip, you were out of luck. Mrs. Mead put her hand over the top of the pitcher and shook it up and down, then placed it in the middle of her desk.

"We'll do the boys first," she said. "All the boys who signed up to be hosts, please come up to my desk and draw a slip of paper."

2

"No need for a stampede," she added as Mark Freedman, Larry Jackson, Pete Stone, Henry Larkin, Donny McElroy, and Steven Gitten jostled each other in a scramble across the room.

Mark got there first. He stuck his hand into the pitcher, felt around, and pulled out a slip of paper. He unfolded it . . . "Alllll right!" he exclaimed. "Austin Albers. I hope he's a good baseball player." Some of the boys in our school have a game every Saturday.

"I hope he's a good student," Mrs. Mead said with a smile. "Steven?"

Steven Gitten drew a blank slip. Disgusted, he wadded it up and threw it into the wastebasket. Then Larry Jackson drew a boy named Jim Klager. Donny drew the second blank piece of paper. Pete's slip said Tommy Nixon, and Henry Larkin ended up with a boy named Reggie Bennett.

"Our turn!" Kate whispered to me — we sit next to each other in the second row. "I hope all four of us get somebody!"

"Girls?" said Mrs. Mead after she'd shaken up eight more slips in the clay pitcher.

Besides Kate, Stephanie, Patti, and me, Nancy Hersh, Jane Sykes, Jenny Carlin, and Jenny's sidekick, Angela Kemp, lined up to draw for the five girl visitors.

Nancy was at the head of the line. She unfolded her slip of paper and made a face, because her slip was blank. "Nuts!" Nancy muttered.

"She was looking forward to a girl in the house," Kate whispered. Nancy has three brothers.

Stephanie drew next. She crossed her eyes for extra good luck and stuck her fingers into the pitcher. She opened her slip of paper so fast that she ripped it in half. There was definitely writing on it. Stephanie held the two halves together and read out loud: "Molly Jones!"

Jane Sykes drew a girl named Carol Harrison.

Then it was Kate's turn. She unfolded her piece of paper carefully. . . . "Darlene Kastner!" she said with a smile, stepping out of the way so I could draw.

I held my breath while I dug into the jar and pulled open my slip. "I got one!" I hissed to Kate. "Annette Hollis," I told Mrs. Mead, who was keeping a list of who'd drawn whom.

There was only one girl from Walden left, and three girls to draw for her. Stephanie, Kate, and I watched as Patti shuffled the slips around with her fingers before pulling one out. She unfolded it, then shook her head glumly. Patti had come up with a blank.

"That's okay," Stephanie whispered to her. "You and I can share Molly."

"And Darlene," said Kate.

"And Annette," I added.

Kate, Stephanie, Patti, and I are best friends. Besides doing just about everything else together, we take turns sleeping over at one another's houses every Friday. We load up on junk food, read movie and teen magazines, watch triple features on TV, try out new hairstyles, practice dance steps, and play crazy games of Truth or Dare, among other things. Our four-girl sleepovers are Friday-night institutions.

Of course, there haven't always been four of us, or even three of us. The sleepovers started years ago with just Kate and me. I think one reason Kate and I have stayed friends for so long is that we're so different. I'm tall, she's short; I'm dark, she's blonde. I like sports, she'd rather not get hot and sweaty. Kate's always sensible, and sometimes I have a runaway imagination, I'll have to admit. I like to think I loosen her up a little. She definitely settles me down.

Another reason we're friends is, we're practically next-door neighbors on Pine Street. There's just one house between us. Kate and I have known each other since we were in diapers and have played together almost every day since we were toddlers. Then, in kindergarten, we started spending Friday nights with each other. Either I'd sleep over at Kate's house, or she'd sleep over at mine. Dr. Beekman, Kate's dad, named us the Sleepover Twins.

There were no teen magazines or new hairstyles or dance steps at our sleepovers in those days, since we were only five at the time. We did a lot of dressing up in our moms' clothes and pretending we were grown-ups. And we ate a lot of cherry Kool-Pops in warm weather or s'mores melted in a toaster-oven on cooler nights.

As we got older, we got much more serious about our Friday-night munchies. Kate started making her super-fudge, and I invented my special dip of onion soup, olives, bacon bits, and sour cream. We plowed through bushels of barbecue potato chips and guzzled gallons of Dr Pepper.

There was my older brother, Roger, and his friends to spy on, and Kate's little sister, Melissa the Monster, to steer clear of, and hundreds of games of Mad Libs. But it was still just the two of us — Kate and me.

Then Stephanie showed up in Mr. Civello's room, my fourth-grade class. It turned out she'd just moved from the city to the other end of Pine Street. Stephanie told neat stories about city life; she knew a lot about the latest styles, and she was a great dancer — I really thought she was fun. After I'd known Stephanie for a month or two, I asked Kate if it would be all right to invite her to one of our sleep-overs. Kate said yes.

It wasn't exactly like at first sight between Kate and Stephanie. Kate thought Stephanie was an air-head, with all her talk about clothes and shopping, and Stephanie thought Kate was a stuffy know-it-all.

My brother said they were too much alike, both of them used to bossing people around. I didn't give up, though, because I wanted them to be friends, too. I invited Stephanie again. Then she asked Kate and me to a sleepover at her house — Mrs. Green made great peanut butter-chocolate chip cookies. Finally, Stephanie and Kate began to understand each other a little better.

Last September, all three of us ended up in Mrs. Mead's fifth-grade class. So did Patti Jenkins. Her family had moved to Riverhurst from the city in the summer, although you'd never guess she'd ever lived there. Patti's as quiet and shy as Stephanie is gabby and outgoing, but they actually lived in the same city neighborhood for a while and went to the same school in kindergarten and first grade.

Stephanie wanted Patti to be part of our gang. Kate and I did, too. Both us liked Patti right away, and soon there were *four* Sleepover Friends.

As soon as Mrs. Mead had announced the exchange with Walden, the four of us hoped we would all end up with a visitor. We'd even planned an eight-girl sleepover in Patti's attic for the following Friday, after the party at school, and I think Patti felt she'd let us down. "Sorry, guys," she mumbled unhappily.

"Hey, listen — isn't seven a lucky number? We're going to have a great week!" I whispered.

The worst thing about Patti drawing a blank slip, as far as I was concerned, was that Jenny Carlin or Angela Kemp would end up with the last Walden girl.

Jenny Carlin is small and dark, with a high, whiny voice. I never had a problem with her before this year, but she's gotten absolutely boy crazy, which is the main reason she and I don't get along. At the beginning of this year, Jenny decided she liked Pete Stone. In the lunchroom, on the playground, after school, she'd hang on his every word. Then, for a while at least, Pete Stone seemed to be liking me — sitting at our lunch-table and talking to me before school started in the morning, stuff like that.

Although I wasn't trying to make Pete like me, Jenny's never forgiven me for it. She just imagines everyone's as nuts over boys as she is.

Ever since then, Jenny loves it if she thinks she's put one over on me, or any of the Sleepover Friends.

Stephanie poked me with her elbow. Jenny had her fingers stuck in the clay pitcher and was really taking her time.

"Draw, already," Kate muttered.

Finally, Jenny pulled a slip out. She opened it and looked at it for a few seconds, smiling smugly. Then she turned the slip around so Angela — and just coincidentally the rest of us — could see it. "Rebecca Newman," Jenny said, a satisfied smirk on her little face.

Chapter 2

"Jenny Carlin burns me up! Lauren, grab that bag of chips off the counter," Stephanie said. That Friday, the sleepover was at her house, and the four of us were in the kitchen gathering supplies for a serious night of TV-watching in Stephanie's room. "Jenny and Angela didn't even sign up for a guest until they saw that we had!" Stephanie went on.

"I really feel sorry for her," Kate said, picking up a bottle of Cherry Coke and one of Dr Pepper.

"Who? Jenny Carlin?" I squawked.

Kate raised a blonde eyebrow at me. "No, silly, the poor Walden girl who has to spend the week with Jenny."

"Rebecca Newman," said Patti, who hardly

10

ever forgets anything. Patti's one of the smartest kids in the fifth grade. "Her name is Rebecca Newman. I wonder what she's like?" Patti was probably thinking of Rebecca as the guest *she* should have had.

"She'd better be tough, or Jenny will run right over her," said Stephanie. "Jenny may look dainty, but she's got the personality of a bulldozer. All set?" she asked us.

Kate had the bottles of soda under her arms, and she was holding a big bowl of the dip Patti learned to make on her trip to Alaska (tuna, catsup, cream cheese, and some other stuff mixed in a blender). Patti was carrying some of the Greens' leftover Chinese spareribs on a platter.

Stephanie had the tray with ice-filled glasses, paper napkins, bowls, and plates on it. I picked up a giant bag of onion-and-sour-cream potato skins.

Then I noticed a brown bag on the floor next to the kitchen table. "Anything for the sleepover in here?" I asked Stephanie.

She shook her head. "No. Those are old books Mom's taking to the library sale," Stephanie answered.

I dropped the potato skins on the table and reached into the bag. I read the title of the book on

11

the top of the pile: "*Body Talks*. Is your mom getting into exercise, Stephanie?" I probably sounded a little surprised, because Stephanie would rather give up eating completely than sweat. I figured like daughter, like mother.

"No," Stephanie said. "It's not an exercise book. It's about body language — how your body shows what your thoughts are." She shifted her hands on the tray she was holding. "Come on, Lauren. This is getting heavy."

"Sounds interesting. . . ." I started flipping through the book.

"Sounds sort of like mind-reading to me," Kate said with a sniff. "Lauren, put that book down before you get any funny ideas!"

Kate's always teasing me for letting my imagination run away with me, just because I don't laugh at astrology, or fortune-telling, or the Ouija board. Can anybody *prove* they don't work?

"It's not like mind-reading at all." Stephanie rested the tray on the kitchen table and took the book from me. "Actually, it's kind of scientific. You can figure out what people are thinking and feeling from the way they're standing or sitting, or holding their arms — even if they don't ever open their mouth."

12

Kate shook her head. "Give me a break!"

"Like you, for example," Stephanie said with a grin. "You're standing there shaking your head. Your body language tells me that you don't believe this book for a minute."

Kate jerked her hand away from her hip and frowned. "Well, if that's all there is to it. . . ."

I took the book back. "Wait a second." I turned to a photograph of a man sitting in a chair. "See this? He's got his arms and legs crossed, which means he doesn't want anybody getting closer to him."

"He could say the same thing a lot more easily by simply sticking out his tongue, couldn't he?" Patti said very seriously.

Then she giggled, and all of us cracked up.

"Could we get going, or did you want to spend the entire sleepover in the kitchen, Lauren?" Stephanie said.

"Yeah, the movie's about to start," Kate said.

Kate's a real movie freak: old movies, new ones, foreign films, musicals — you name it, Kate'll watch it. She wants to be a movie director some day. And she hates missing even the opening credits.

"All right, all right," I said. I picked up the chips again, but I brought the book along, too.

We followed Stephanie down the hall to her room. It's decorated in her favorite color combination: red, black, and white. The bedspreads on the twin beds have red, black, and white stripes. The two foam-rubber, fold-out chairs are covered in red denim. Even Stephanie's kitten matches — Cinders is coal black.

He was asleep on the black-and-white rug in front of the television set. Stephanie's an only child, and she has her own TV and phone.

Stephanie put the tray down on her desk and flipped on the TV. Kate dug her glasses out of her backpack and slipped them on in time to see the title of the movie, *Sunshine Beach*. Kate's near-sighted, but she only wears her glasses if something's really important.

Keeping an eye on the screen, we poured soda into glasses of ice, grabbed the munchies, and sprawled on the rug next to Cinders.

" 'Starring Kevin DeSpain and Tanya Colter,' " Kate read out loud. "I think they'll be excellent together."

Kevin DeSpain is our favorite actor. He's one of the stars of *Made for Each Other*, on channel 6 every Tuesday night. He's also been in lots of movies.

"Kevin is *so* cute," Patti said.

"And so tall," I added. I'm the tallest girl in fifth grade, next to Patti. Height matters as much to me as Kevin's dark wavy hair, green eyes, and adorable dimples . . . almost.

"According to *Star Turns* magazine, he has definitely broken up with Marcy Monroe" — Marcy's a star on "Made," too — "and he's apparently been dating Tanya since then," Stephanie reported.

"If he and Tanya are actually going together, when they kiss they'll really mean it!" Patti said, giving Cinders a big kiss.

As soon as the credits were over, Tanya Colter appeared on the screen. She was lying on a towel at the beach, wearing a tiny white two-piece bathing suit and big green sunglasses.

Stephanie swallowed a mound of dip balanced on a potato skin and groaned. "I'd kill for those cheekbones," she said, sucking in her own cheeks until she resembled Donald Duck. "I'm starting a serious diet right now!"

"More for me," I said, grabbing a sparerib. Stephanie's always starting serious diets. She's short, and a little curvy, with curly black hair and dark eyes. But even if she dieted for the rest of her life, I don't think she could look like Tanya Colter, who's tall and lanky, with straight blonde hair sort of like Kate's.

"Here comes Kevin!" Patti squeaked.

Kevin DeSpain strolled onto the screen in an electric-blue bathing suit with a bright yellow stripe running across it. His hair was sun-streaked and a little longer than usual, and it was brushed back from his face with mousse.

"Wow!" all four of us shrieked at once.

Kevin was smiling that sort of half-smile, half-frown that makes him so lovable and staring straight at Tanya.

"If I were Tanya, I'd definitely faint," said Stephanie, absentmindedly scooping up another load of Alaska dip with a chip. She washed it down with a big slug of Cherry Coke and grabbed a sparerib, never taking her eyes off the television screen.

"Mmmm-hmmm," Patti agreed dreamily.

But Tanya didn't faint. In fact, even though her lips smiled invitingly at Kevin, she folded her arms firmly across the top of her two-piece.

"Look at that!" I exclaimed, grabbing *Body Talks* and opening it to the photos in the middle. "According to the book, Tanya wants Kevin to leave her alone. Just like this picture — "

"Ssssh! Could I please listen to what she's saying?" Kate frowned at me and hopped up to raise the volume on the TV.

"Where have you been, stranger?" Tanya purred, smiling up at Kevin.

"Around," Kevin replied, digging the toes of one foot into the sand.

"I've missed you, Paul," said Tanya in her hoarse, breathy voice.

"I've missed you, Paul." Stephanie tried to sound hoarse and breathy around a mouthful of dip. "It doesn't seem to me that she wants him to leave her alone."

I pointed out a picture in the book of a girl standing next to a boy, her arms crossed like Tanya's. "Your voice can lie, but not your body," I argued. "It says so right here. Listen: 'Crossed legs and arms and not meeting a person's eyes signal that you want the person to stay away.' Under those sunglasses, she's probably not even looking at him."

I snapped the book closed. "The *movie* may be about Tanya liking Kevin, but I don't think she likes him at all in *real life*!"

"Ssssh!" Kate hissed again. She's very serious

about movies — she even gets upset when we talk during the commercial breaks.

But it was hard for me to get interested in what was happening on the TV screen, now that I knew how Tanya really felt about Kevin. So I opened *Body Talks* again and kept reading.

I found out as I read on that there are also signals to let people know you do like them. Like tilting your head (I'd seen Jenny Carlin do that to Pete Stone a hundred times) or batting your lashes (ditto). "Hey, have you guys ever seen me do anything like batting my lashes?" Maybe body language could tell you things you didn't even know about yourself.

Kate, Stephanie, and Patti weren't paying any attention to me. They were glued to the TV and *Sunshine Beach*.

I was pretty sure I'd never batted my lashes at any boy — the very idea was totally embarrassing! But after I'd read some more of the book, I began to wonder: Just *leaning forward* was a way of encouraging people, it said, and so was *nodding*.

Had I ever leaned forward or nodded at Pete? Or at Mark Freedman or Larry Jackson? Or worse, at Robert Ellwanger, the biggest nerd at Riverhurst Elementary? Had they ever nodded at me? Had I seen

Stephanie, or Kate, or Patti doing those things?

The others watched the movie to the end, but I couldn't tear myself away from *Body Talks*. I read it right through, cover to cover. I knew one thing when I was finished — I was going to start watching myself *and* everybody else.

"Think of all the people we've given the wrong impression to," I said when Stephanie had switched off the set. "Leaning, smiling, nodding. . . ."

"Cinders has his paw over his nose," Kate said to Stephanie. "Do you think that means he doesn't like us?" she snickered.

"Or that he thinks we smell?" Stephanie giggled.

Patti leaned closer to the kitten, who was stretched out on one of the beds. "He's snoring," she announced.

"Lauren, you're letting your imagination run away with you again. . . ," Kate warned. "I hope you keep a grip on yourself in front of . . . what's your Walden girl's name?"

"Annette," I said. If they weren't going to take *Body Talks* seriously, I was glad to change the subject. "I know we're planning to give the Walden girls a bike tour of Riverhurst and go to Charlie's Soda Fountain the first chance we get" — Charlie's has

19

the best ice-cream in town — "and to the school party, and to Patti's for the sleepover, but that won't take all week. What else are we supposed to do with them?"

"Mrs. Mead said to show them how we live, what our interests are," Stephanie replied. "I think I'll take Molly to the mall and go shopping at Just Juniors and Dandelion, for starters." Those are kids' clothing boutiques — they're practically second homes for Stephanie.

"What if she doesn't have any money to spend?" Patti asked. "Won't she feel uncomfortable?"

"Not at all. We'll just try things on," Stephanie said. "There probably aren't any nice clothes to look at in a little farm town — it'll be educational for her."

"Well, I'm going to rent all my favorite movies, and Darlene and I will watch them on Dad's new VCR," Kate said.

Poor Darlene. One of Kate's favorite movies is fifty years old, three and a half hours long, in black and white, and all the actors speak Russian!

"Sounds like a lot of fun," I said. "I'm going to take Annette jogging on the special course at Riverhurst Park. I bet farm kids are in super shape. And maybe we'll go hiking in the Wildlife Refuge — you can come with us, Patti."

"What about swimming laps at the indoor pool at the university?" Patti suggested. Patti's parents teach history there.

"You're going to wear Annette completely out!" Stephanie said. She and Kate are always teasing Patti and me about what jocks we are.

"Yeah, she'll be glad to get back to the farm. Milking hundreds of cows would be a lot more relaxing than running her legs off," Kate said.

"I'm sure everyone will have a terrific time," Patti said quickly, while I was still thinking of a smart answer. Patti's good at heading off arguments.

"It'll be like having a week-long sleepover!" I exclaimed. "I can't wait!"

"I can't, either," said Stephanie. "In less than forty-eight hours, we'll be meeting their bus in front of the school." She swept the dip bowl clean with a potato skin. "How much weight can I lose between Saturday morning and Sunday afternoon?"

Chapter 3

The next morning, I found out I wasn't the only one who took *Body Talks* seriously. Stephanie's dad is a lawyer and he'd bought the book to help him figure out whether or not people were telling the truth in the courtroom. Mr. Green had read *Body Talks* three times and gone on to buy *Body Conversations*, which is newer and bigger.

"Keep the book, Lauren," he said while Mrs. Green was making waffles for us all. "You may learn things about your friends, new *and* old, you wouldn't ever have known otherwise."

Stephanie and Kate just nudged each other and giggled.

By the time breakfast was finished, it had started

to rain, so Mr. Green drove us all to our houses.

I had planned to clean up my room for Annette that Saturday. As Kate, who is super neat, would be quick to tell you, I'm sort of a messy person. Since it rained all day, I should have had plenty of time to make things absolutely perfect.

Instead, I drove with my dad to his office — Blaney Realty. I helped him redo his files and fiddled around with the computer. That evening, the whole family went out to the Burger Joint at the mall. When we got back home, I had to read the issue of *Reel News* that I'd picked up at Fred's Magazines.

I tore the main article out to show to Kate, Stephanie, and Patti: "Kevin and Tanya On the Outs." It told about the "on-again, off-again romance of Kevin DeSpain and Tanya Colter," which, it just so happened, was definitely *off* when they made *Sunshine Beach* together. "Filming was interrupted by constant bickering on the set," *Reel News* reported.

See? I thought, they really weren't getting along. Which proves that *Body Talks* was right after all!

Anyway, I stayed up late reading *Reel News* and comparing photos of people in the magazine with photos in *Body Talks* to figure out what they were really up to. Then I overslept Sunday morning. I didn't wake up until my mother knocked on my door with a chore for me.

"Lauren, I think you could make the visit a lot more pleasant for Annette if you bathed Bullwinkle," she suggested. "He's awfully muddy from the rain yesterday."

"Urgh . . . ," I muttered, burying my head under my pillow. "Where's Roger?"

After all, Bullwinkle is basically Roger's dog. My brother was five when he picked Bullwinkle out at the animal shelter.

Bullwinkle was once a black, furry little puppy. "Mostly cocker spaniel," the people at the shelter told my parents. "He won't get very large."

As compared to what? An elephant? Bullwinkle now weighs a hundred thirty pounds, and he's over five feet tall when he stands up on his hind legs. A dog that size covered with mud is not an attractive picture.

"Roger's at the track meet," Mom said.

"Annette's a farm kid," I grumbled, pulling my covers tighter. "She's probably used to cleaning out barns and stuff. One muddy dog won't bother her."

"Lauren . . . ," said my mother in her *right now* tone of voice.

"Okay, okay. . . ." I said, sitting up slowly.

"I think you can get your dad to help you," Mom told me.

So Dad and I spent the rest of the morning wrestling with Bullwinkle, first trying to get the dog soap on him, and then trying to get it off.

We cleaned ourselves up, ate lunch, and watched a tennis match.

"I took a look at your room, Lauren . . . ," my mom said as Roy Burke slammed the ball across the net past Dan Klass. She shook her head and sighed.

"I'll straighten it up in a second, Mom," I said. "As soon as this match is over."

I ended up with just enough time to make up my bed and cram all of the clutter into my desk, my chest-of-drawers, and my closet before I had to go pick up Annette. I fluffed up the pillows and scooped up Rocky, my black-and-white kitten — brother to Stephanie's kitten, Cinders; Patti's Adelaide; and Kate's Fredericka — and put him on the bottom bunk. My room looked fine, as long as Annette didn't open anything. What she didn't know wouldn't hurt her, right?

Then a horn honked three times outside. Mrs. Beekman was driving Kate and me to meet the Walden bus. I stuck my head out the window to yell, "Be right down!"

I hurried downstairs, said good-bye to my parents, and raced to Mrs. Beekman's car.

Kate was sitting up front with her mother. As I climbed into the back seat she turned around. "You dressed down, too," Kate said, nodding approvingly at my second-best sweater, green with buttons down the left shoulder, my black sweats, and jogging shoes.

"Yeah. I thought of what Stephanie said, about the Walden kids probably not having too many good places to shop. I didn't want to make anybody feel funny," I said.

"Me, neither," said Kate. She had on a T-shirt, her blue cardigan, and her favorite stone-washed jeans. She checked her watch. "I hope we're not late," she said.

That's another way Kate and I are different. She's always early, and I'm usually the opposite.

"We have plenty of time," Mrs. Beekman told her.

Stephanie was already waiting when we drove up to the school. She waved from her father's car and climbed out to meet us.

"I bet I can guess how Stephanie spent *her* Saturday," Kate murmured to me.

Stephanie was wearing a brand-new outfit: a bright-red cable-knit sweater, black denim overalls, and spotless white sneakers. "To make the Walden kids feel at home," she explained when she saw us checking out her clothes. "You know — overalls, farming?"

"Right," said Kate, raising an eyebrow at me.

We said hi to Mrs. Mead, who was talking to Mrs. Jackson and Mrs. Freedman near the bike rack. Then we sat down on the bench next to the sidewalk.

"Did you see Jenny?" Stephanie pointed her chin in the direction of the school building.

Jenny Carlin was perched on the steps, wearing a bright-pink jumpsuit, her hair pulled into a ponytail on the top of her head with a matching pink ribbon. She was blabbing away to Mark Freedman and Pete Stone, natch.

She was also batting her eyelashes, tilting her head, leaning, and nodding. It was incredible! She looked like four illustrations from *Body Talks* rolled into one. Actually, the way she was bouncing around, she looked more like a pinball machine. I halfway expected to see her eyes light up and hear a bell go off!

Kate must have been thinking along the same lines, because she muttered, "Jenny had better watch it, or she'll blow a fuse!"

"Have you talked to Patti?" I asked Stephanie.

"Yes. I told her Dad and Molly and I would pick her up and we'd go for pizza," Stephanie said. "Hey, why don't you guys come, too?"

"That's a great idea!" I said. I'd have to call home, but my parents wouldn't mind. We were planning to have roast beef sandwiches and potato salad for dinner, which Annette and I could eat the next day if we wanted.

"Sure, we can all get to know each other together," said Kate.

Then Larry Jackson yelled, "There's the bus!"

Chapter
4

Way down Mill Road, a small bus, about the size of a large van, was coming into view. Kate, Stephanie, and I jumped to our feet and stared as it chugged toward us.

As the bus pulled up in front of the school, we could see the kids inside it staring back at us through the windows.

The bus driver put on the brakes and opened the door, and a pretty woman with short, brown hair stepped out.

"Ms. Powell," Kate guessed.

Sure enough, Mrs. Mead ran to meet the woman, and they gave each other a big hug.

Stephanie squeezed my arm. "Here they come," she said.

The first kid off the bus was tall and solid-looking, with reddish-blond hair and freckles. The Riverhurst boys crowded close enough to read the nametag he was wearing on his jacket.

"Yo, Austin!" Mark Freedman said happily, slapping him on the back — I guess he thought Austin Albers looked like a baseball player. "I'm Mark. You're staying with me!"

Pete Stone said hello to Tommy Nixon, a thin boy with huge hands and feet. Larry Jackson hooked up with Jim Klager, a short, friendly looking guy with curly brown hair.

Then Stephanie gave me a sharp jab in the ribs. "Hunk-and-a-half!" she whispered.

The last Walden boy off the bus had spiky blond hair, pale blue eyes, and a light tan. He was wearing shades on a cord, a brown bomber jacket, and a great smile. Stephanie wasn't exaggerating. He was the kind of boy everyone agrees is cute, no matter how different their opinions usually are.

He'd turned around to say something to the girl stepping out of the bus behind him, when Henry

Larkin spoke up. "Reggie? I'm Henry Larkin, so you'll be staying at my house."

"Hi, Henry." Reggie Bennett shook Henry's hand. Then he introduced the girl. "This is Rebecca Newman. We're first cousins."

Oh, no! Rebecca Newman was Jenny's visitor! Stephanie, Kate, and I all groaned at about the same time that Jenny leapt forward. She practically knocked Henry out of the way to collect her prize.

"Rebecca Newman?" she cooed, hardly taking her eyes off Reggie Bennett for a second. "I'm Jenny Carlin, and I'm really happy that *you'll* be my guest for the week."

Jenny leaned so far toward Reggie, I thought she might tip over.

"Jenny, this is my cousin, Reggie Bennett," Rebecca said politely. She probably got this kind of reaction to her gorgeous cousin all the time.

Rebecca herself was thin, with straight brown hair held back with clips and a serious expression. In fact, she reminded me a little of Patti, especially in the days before she opened up and we really got to know her well.

"Jenny's going to run all over her," Kate predicted.

"Jenny has to *notice* her first," Stephanie said.

Jenny was gushing over Reggie and grinning like a cat that just swallowed *forty* canaries.

"It's such a shame," Stephanie said.

"What is?" Kate asked.

"If she doesn't give him some room, she's going to drool all over that nice jacket." Kate looked disgusted, but I wasn't sure if it was with Jenny or with Stephanie.

Just then, another girl stepped down. Her long, dark hair swished in a ponytail down her back. "Carol Harrison," her nametag said — she belonged to Jane Sykes for the week.

Carol had on a really nice navy plaid jacket, a short skirt, and tights. Rebecca Newman was wearing jeans, a green-and-yellow zigzagged sweater, and canvas boots.

"They're all dressed much nicer than we are," I pointed out to Kate. So much for Stephanie's idea about poorly clothed farm kids!

Stephanie just nodded. She was watching the third girl getting off the bus. "This one *has* to be Molly!" she said positively.

The girl had black hair in a braid and round glasses with red frames. She was wearing high-waisted black pants with yellow suspenders, a white sweatshirt with yellow polka-dots, and yellow sneakers with a red stripe around the soles. Sure enough, she announced, "I'm Molly Jones," as Stephanie rushed up to her.

"I'm Stephanie Green," Stephanie said. "I know we're going to have a fabulous week!"

"They look like twins who were separated at birth," Kate said. "The Shopping Sisters."

With Stephanie paired off, everybody was taken care of except Kate and me.

The last two girls climbed down from the bus and glanced around for their hostesses. One was about my height, with short, wavy hair, and kind of a bouncy step. She was wearing jeans and Mercury jogging shoes, exactly like mine.

The other girl was shorter, about the same size as Kate. Her blonde hair was blunt cut, and she wore a turquoise-blue sweater and skirt, pink tights, and loafers, all very neat.

"The girl in the jogging shoes must be Annette," I said hopefully.

"Right," said Kate, heading toward the other girl.

When we'd gotten closer, though, we saw that

the opposite was true. Annette was the short, neat one. The girl in jogging shoes was Kate's visitor, Darlene Kastner. And if I was reading their body talk correctly, the Walden girls didn't like each other one bit! They'd turned their backs to each other, even though they were standing only a foot or two apart.

Darlene saw me first. She looked down at my feet in their Mercurys, and her face lit up. "Do I go with you?" she asked.

I shook my head. "No, Annette Hollis does." I introduced myself. "I'm Lauren Hunter, and this is my friend, Kate Beekman. You're staying at her house." There was a flicker of disappointment in Darlene's eyes. I was disappointed myself, because she looked like fun. At least she was staying practically next door. Darlene grinned and said hi to Kate.

The last girl, who had to be Annette Hollis by process of elimination, was still standing with her back to us. She didn't look even a little curious about finding her hostess. I tapped her on the shoulder.

She whirled around, scowling so fiercely that I jumped.

"Annette? I'm Lauren Hunter," I said quickly.

"And?" she asked. Brrr. Her voice was so cold,

I felt as if the temperature had suddenly dropped twenty degrees.

"You'll be staying with me," I explained, beginning to feel a little silly.

"Oh," Annette said, with a sideways glare toward Darlene.

I looked around. Rebecca and Jenny, Molly and Stephanie, Darlene and Kate, and all the boys were blabbing away. For some reason I couldn't think of another thing to say to Annette. Maybe it was that frown that didn't go away.

Luckily, Mrs. Mead started clapping her hands together to get everyone's attention. "I see that you've sorted yourselves out," she said with a smile. "I just wanted to welcome the Walden fifth-graders. I know we'll have a wonderful week, and I'll see you all in class tomorrow."

"Kids, please collect your luggage," Ms. Powell added, "because Gus and I have to start back." Gus was the bus driver.

Everybody moved toward the rear of the bus, where Gus had piled the suitcases on the sidewalk. Everybody except my guest, Annette, that is. She hung back as though the whole thing were a big bore.

"Hey, Lauren. What's happening?" It was Pete Stone, walking beside us with Tommy Nixon.

I saw Jenny Carlin's head swivel in my direction as soon as Pete spoke. She had Reggie Bennett right next to her, but I guess one boy wasn't enough.

If Jenny thought I was going to act all flirty and stupid the way she did, she had another thing coming! Remembering what I had read in *Body Talks*, I leaned as far away from Pete as I could, crossed my arms, and peered at the ground. "Hello, Pete," I mumbled.

I could feel his puzzled stare. Stephanie called out, "Lauren — over here!"

"Come on, Annette," I said, and I pushed my way through the crowd to the suitcases.

Molly and Darlene had already gotten theirs. Stephanie introduced me to Molly, and I introduced her to Annette, who was lurking behind me.

"How do you want to get to Mimi's? Should we all try to squeeze into Dad's car?" Stephanie asked. "We're going to Mimi's Pizza for an early dinner," she explained to the Walden girls. "I hope everybody's hungry."

"You bet," said Molly. "Although I probably should be dieting . . . I could always have salad . . .

36

or not eat the cheese . . . or . . ." She and Stephanie were a perfect match!

"I'm starving!" Darlene exclaimed.

So was I — one of Mimi's stuffed pizzas would really hit the spot.

"Since you have to pick up Patti," Kate said to Stephanie, "Annette, Lauren, Darlene, and I should go in my mom's car. We'll meet you at Mimi's."

"Okay," Stephanie said. "Give us ten or fifteen minutes." She picked up Molly's suitcase and hurried toward Mr. Green's car.

"That's us, the white car over there," Kate said to Darlene and Annette.

Just as I was about to say I needed to call home, Annette finally spoke. "I'd rather not go for pizza, if you don't mind," she announced from behind me.

"You don't like pizza?" Kate turned to look at her, flabbergasted.

I wasn't as surprised by what Annette had said as Kate was. After all, I'd read *Body Talks* cover to cover. I wasn't sure pizza had anything to do with it.

I saw Darlene roll her eyes when Annette answered primly, "I'm not feeling very well — I get carsick."

Kate looked at me and raised an eyebrow.

I shrugged my shoulders. "Would you mind giving us a ride home before you go to Mimi's?" I asked her.

"Of course not," said Kate. She grabbed Darlene's suitcase and marched toward the car with her guest. I could tell Kate was annoyed at Annette by how stiffly she was holding her shoulders.

Annette reached for her own suitcase — blue tweed with brown trim. Without saying another word, she started after them.

I sighed. I had a feeling it was going to be a very long week.

Chapter
5

I felt pretty gloomy on the way to my house. Kate and Darlene sat in front and talked about a science-fiction movie they'd both seen on TV. Annette and I sat in back with the two suitcases and didn't say anything.

"We'll have a pizza with everything in your honor at Mimi's," Kate said as Mrs. Beekman turned into my driveway. She was trying to cheer me up.

"Thanks — see you tomorrow morning," I told her. "Eight-fifteen, at my mailbox," Kate said.

As soon as Mrs. Beekman stopped the car, Annette piled out and yanked out her suitcase.

"Good-bye, Annette," Kate said coolly.

"Good-bye." Annette was fidgeting impatiently on the sidewalk.

I waved as Mrs. Beekman backed down the driveway to the street.

"Do your parents take you to school, or do you and Kate go on the bus?" Annette asked as we headed for the front steps.

"Neither. We ride our bikes," I said, "and we've got enough for you guys."

Kate, Stephanie, Patti, and I always ride together to school and back on our bikes. We'd managed to scrounge up extra bicycles for the Walden visitors so they could ride, too.

I was planning to use Roger's old bike myself, and lend mine to Annette. Kate had borrowed a bike from Donald Foster, the seventh-grader who lives in the house between Kate's and mine. And Stephanie already had two bikes, last year's five-speed and this year's twelve-speed.

But Annette frowned and shook her head. "I can't possibly ride a bike," she said. "I had a serious accident on one not long ago, and I'm not supposed to even get *near* a bike for at least six more months."

"Oh." *Bummer!* No rides to school with Kate,

Stephanie, and Patti, no bike tour of Riverhurst with the Waldenites. And if Annette and Darlene didn't straighten out their problems, no Charlie's Soda Fountain with the gang, probably no school party, and definitely no sleepover at Patti's on Friday, either!

"Well," I said. "In that case, my mom will take us to school and pick us up."

Then I threw open the front door. I wasn't thinking about Bullwinkle.

After he gets bathed, he has to stay inside until he's completely dry so he won't catch cold. Since his fur is so thick, drying can take *hours*. In other words, Bullwinkle was still in the house, instead of outside in the backyard, which is where he usually spends his days.

Annette and I hadn't taken more than a few steps into the hall when he charged out of the dining room, his tail slashing back and forth with excitement. Bullwinkle always has the best intentions, but if you're not expecting a 130-pound dog in your face, I guess he can be sort of frightening.

Anyway, Annette screeched so loudly that both my parents came racing out of the kitchen. I'd thrown my arms around Bullwinkle's neck to keep him away from her, but he outweighs me by a good fifty pounds, so he just dragged me along with him.

He'd almost reached Annette, who was backed up against a wall, holding her suitcase in front of her like a shield, when Dad grabbed his collar.

"Sit, Bullwinkle — *sit!*" Dad commanded.

Occasionally, from somewhere in the back of Bullwinkle's tiny brain, a memory of his obedience lessons ten years ago floats to the surface. I couldn't believe it, but Bullwinkle actually *sat down!*

My mother took Annette's suitcase. She led Annette safely around Bullwinkle and upstairs to my room.

Annette collapsed into the desk chair, which I thought was kind of overreacting for a kid who'd grown up in a farm town.

"Are you all right?" my mother asked her.

"Fine," Annette answered weakly.

"Maybe you'd like to lie down for a few minutes?" Mom suggested.

"The dog . . . ," Annette began.

"We'll take him outside," my mother promised.

Annette nodded and crawled onto the bottom

bunk. She'd hardly lain down when she shrieked and bounded up again.

She'd put her arm down on something black and furry — Rocky, who was asleep on my bed.

By the time Kate called that evening, Rocky had been banished, too, to the spare bedroom.

"What are you doing?" Kate asked.

"You'll never believe it," I whispered into the phone in the hall.

"Try me," said Kate.

"Cleaning out my closet," I said, feeling totally dismal.

"WHAT?" Kate nearly broke my eardrum. "You *never* clean out your closet!"

"I do, too!" I snapped.

"Only when you've lost something," Kate pointed out.

"That's not the worst of it," I added glumly. "After we clean out the closet, we're going to do the the chest-of-drawers and the desk!"

Annette had opened my closet door to hang up some of her neatly folded clothes, and it was all over! Because everything in the closet was really all over — the grungy old sweats I wear jogging with

Roger, a stack of clean T-shirts I couldn't fit in my chest-of-drawers because it was a mess, a jumble of unmatched shoes and sneakers, a pile of movie magazines. . . .

"Do you really read these?" Annette had said, holding up an old issue of *Star Turns* between her thumb and first finger. She made a face, as though it smelled.

"Sometimes . . . ," I'd replied cautiously.

"Well, there's no sense in keeping them once you've read them, is there? You certainly won't need these for school, like *Science Monthly* or something."

Annette had dumped all the magazines into the wastebasket: Good-bye Kevin, good-bye Tanya, good-bye all you stars. . . .

I was just thinking that maybe I could rescue them after Annette went to sleep that night, when Kate suddenly giggled on her end of the line. "Do you know what Darlene calls her?"

"Who?"

"Annette! Little Miss Muffet!"

I could understand why, with Annette practically fainting at the sight of *Rocky*! Forget about Bullwinkle: She was at death's door with Bullwinkle. The business with the bike was weird, too.

Oh! I hadn't told Kate yet. "Listen," I whispered, "Annette says she had a bad bike accident, so she can't ride for a while, which means Mom will be driving the two of us to and from school all this week. . . ."

"Oh, really?" Kate sniffed. "I don't know when Annette could have had a biking accident. Darlene and Molly said she *never* rides a bike when we told them about riding to school. Darlene says Annette stays home all the time, because she thinks she's too good for the other Walden kids!"

"Then why — ?" I started to ask why Annette bothered to be a part of the exchange program between Walden and Riverhurst — *and* make the week a miserable one for me — when Kate interrupted.

"In fact, Darlene said the only reason Annette came on this trip at all is that her father is the school superintendent in Walden. He probably thought it would look bad if she didn't participate."

"Isn't she friends with anybody? Carol Harrison, maybe?" I asked hopefully.

Carol was staying with Jane Sykes. Since I like Jane a lot, I thought the four of us could do some stuff together.

"I don't think so," Kate replied. "Darlene and Molly said Annette moved to Walden this year, and she hasn't tried to get to know anyone. Plus, she shows off in class — she likes to make everybody else feel like a dummy. And she told Darlene that sports and games are stupid!"

"Great!" I groaned. Annette Hollis was a real pill, and I was stuck with her for a whole week: 7 days — It took me a minute to figure out — 168 hours . . . 10,080 long minutes.

"Lauren?" Annette called out sternly from my room. She must have found the mound of dirty clothes under my bed.

"Gotta go — it's Miss Muffet," I muttered to Kate.

"If it's any help, Stephanie, Patti, and I feel really sorry for you," Kate said. "See you at school."

"Yeah. Thanks." I hung up the phone and walked slowly down the hall.

Maybe if I sleep a lot, I was thinking. I had read about something called a sleep cure in an issue of *Star Turns*. It was part of the Dream Diet. To lose weight, you go to sleep. Wake up seven days later, and you've lost twenty pounds. Maybe I could go to sleep, wake up seven days later, and lose Annette.

"Lauren!" Annette called. "Hurry up! We've got a lot left to do. And you better bring a big garbage bag with you."

Six hundred four thousand, eight hundred seconds. . . .

Chapter 6

When Mom dropped us off at school the next morning, I spotted Stephanie, Kate, and Patti at the bike rack with Molly and Darlene. They were talking and laughing; they seemed to be having a great time. Instead of joining them, I slunk silently behind Annette up the walk to the building.

I didn't notice Pete Stone until he stepped in front of me. "Hi, Lauren. Are you mad at me about something?" he asked.

Pete's tall and nice looking, with curly brown hair and green eyes. He was wearing a faded denim jacket with an eagle on the sleeve that I've always liked.

I almost started talking to him. I was ready to

talk to *anybody* who wasn't Annette. Then, over his left shoulder, I caught sight of Jenny Carlin's interested face. She was standing on the front stoop, craning to hear what Pete was saying. And I could just imagine the snide remarks I'd get later from her. I thought of *Body Talks* and her performance the day before. Then I thought, what if somebody saw *me* talking to Pete and got the same impression?

Meanwhile, Pete was waiting for an answer. I quickly looked down at the ground, and leaned away from him. "No . . . of course not," I replied in a low voice. "We're going to be late. . . ." And I darted around him and through the front door of the school.

"You always seem to be running away from that boy," Annette said, scurrying down the hall after me. "Is there something wrong with him?"

"No . . . ," I said. "It's a long story."

"Hello, girls." Mrs. Mead was already sitting at her desk in 5B. She glanced down at the list in front of her. "Hello, Annette. Welcome to our class."

Annette nodded and smiled, for the first time since I'd met her. Did superintendents' daughters only smile at teachers?

"How do you like Riverhurst so far?" Mrs. Mead asked her.

"Just fine." Annette beamed enthusiastically at Mrs. Mead, although as far as I could recall, just about all she'd seen of Riverhurst was the inside of my closet!

"Well, I'm looking forward to hearing about Walden, and I know my students are, too," Mrs. Mead said. "Ms. Powell tells me that the Walden area has more apple orchards and dairy farms than anywhere else in the state!"

Annette nodded, but I would have bet my favorite jeans she didn't know that.

"As part of our social studies classes this week," Mrs. Mead went on, "I'm going to ask each of you visitors to tell us a little about your life in Walden."

Annette's smile clicked off like a light. "I don't really know much about dairy farms or apple orchards," she admitted.

"Then you can tell us anything you'd like to about yourself," Mrs. Mead said. "How you spend your time, the books you like to read, your hobbies. . . ."

Cleaning, I thought.

". . . I'm sure we'll find whatever you have to say interesting. Oh — there's the bell."

Mrs. Mead had borrowed extra desks for some of the visitors, but only four of them would fit in our classroom. Annette, Molly, Darlene, and Carol Harrison took the desks. Rebecca Newman sat at a long table at the back of the room with the four Walden boys.

"She probably wants to get as far away from Jenny Carlin as she can," Kate whispered to me.

Maybe she did. I noticed Rebecca sharing a book with Patti during general science. Patti's desk is at the back of the room, too. Then, during lunch in the cafeteria, Rebecca veered toward Patti's table instead of following Jenny and Angela to theirs.

Jane Sykes and Carol Harrison were sitting with my friends and the other Walden girls, too. But Annette breezed right past them to plunk her tray down on the table in the corner. What could I do? Leave her to eat by herself?

Kate raised an eyebrow. Stephanie called, "Lauren?"

I shrugged my shoulders and trudged after Annette. We ended up only a table away from Jenny

Carlin and Angela, so at least I could see Jenny stare in total disbelief at Rebecca sitting next to Patti.

"Rebecca Newww-mannn!" Jenny hollered, waving her arms. "We're over here!"

Rebecca might have *looked* meek, but she clearly had a mind of her own. She didn't bother to stop talking to Patti long enough even to glance up. When Reggie Bennett sat down next to his cousin and was introduced to Kate, Stephanie, and Patti, I thought Jenny was going to explode!

Watching Jenny's face shading from dead white to pink to beet red put me in a better humor than I'd been in since Annette stepped off the Walden bus. My appetite improved, too.

But I'd barely eaten half my hot dog when Pete Stone dropped into the folding chair across from mine, followed by Tommy Nixon, Mark Freedman, and Austin Albers.

"So, Hunter," Mark Freedman said to me while Pete listened. "Why aren't you talking to Pete? He's a good guy. Don't give him a hard time."

Now Jenny Carlin was glowering at me. She definitely couldn't accuse me of encouraging Pete by leaning and blinking and nodding the way she did. But something had gone wrong with my body talk, because doing the opposite seemed to attract even *more* attention!

Pete was leaning toward me and grinning when Jenny stamped past our table. She stopped just long enough to hiss in my ear, "I know what you're up to, Lauren Hunter! And your friend Patti Jenkins, too!"

Patti Jenkins? I don't think Patti has ever been "up to" anything in her whole life.

I didn't get to talk to Stephanie, Kate, or Patti before lunch was over. Just after lunch, our class has social studies.

"This week, we have an opportunity to learn first-hand about a very different part of our state," Mrs. Mead announced. "At this time each day, I'd like one or two of our Walden visitors to tell us a little about how they live. Do I have any volunteers?"

Several of the boys raised their hands and mumbled about getting it over with.

Mrs. Mead pointed to the sandy-haired boy with freckles. "Austin Albers, isn't it?"

"Yes, ma'am," Austin replied, standing up at

the long table at the back of the room.

"Please come up here, next to my desk, Austin, so we can all hear you."

Austin's family has run a dairy farm since his *great-grandfather* was a boy. Now they have 250 Jersey cows — we found out those are the light-brown kind — that they have to milk every morning and every evening!

Even using milking machines, Austin told us milking the cows takes three hours each time. He has to wake up at quarter to six, seven days a week, school days and weekends, to help his father and his uncle with the chores.

Austin feeds the cows while they're being milked and then gives them more food when they're turned out into a big pen next to the barn. The cows need lots of food to produce seventy pounds of milk a day!

Austin said farming was hard work, but he loved it. He wants to be a dairy farmer, too. For fun, he added, he plays baseball, football, and hockey with his brothers and cousins.

Mark Freedman grinned happily. He could hardly wait until Saturday's baseball game!

When Austin was finished, the Riverhurst kids

asked questions like, What do cows eat? (A lot of grain and grass.) How far did Austin live from school? (About six miles.) Did he own any horses? (No, but his older sister has one.)

While everyone was talking, Stephanie had a chance to turn around in her seat and whisper, "What is going on with you and Pete Stone, Lauren?"

"I was trying to use discouraging body language," I explained in a murmur. "You know — not meeting his gaze, crossing my arms, practically leaning over backwards. But for some reason, it just made him *more* interested in talking to me. I don't understand it!"

"I do," said Stephanie. "He thinks you're a woman of mystery."

"Oh, right." Lauren Hunter, Woman of Mystery. "Ha, ha."

"I'm serious!" Stephanie hissed. "Like in *Sunshine Beach*."

That was the movie I'd missed on Friday, because I was reading *Body Talks*.

"What about it?" I asked.

"Kevin had dumped Tanya Colter, and he only started getting interested in her again when she learned to ignore him," Kate chimed in.

"Girls . . . girls!" said Mrs. Mead. "No talking, please!"

So *Body Talks* said that positive signs would encourage someone's interest. But *Sunshine Beach* suggested that acting negative would make a person seem mysterious and interesting. There was only one thing left for me to do: I'd have to resort to acting like my true self again . . . and see what happened.

Chapter
7

I'd decided how to deal with one problem. But I still had Annette Hollis to worry about.

My mother was waiting for us at the curb after school. She was pretty quiet on the way home. As Annette and I started up the stairs to my room, though, Mom asked, "Lauren, could I talk to you for a moment?"

"Sure. Go ahead," I told Annette. "I'll be right up."

Mom was waiting in the kitchen with a worried frown on her face.

Uh oh. "What did I do?" I asked.

"It's not you, cookie?" Mom replied. "It's Annette."

"What about Annette? Did she make my room so neat that you've decided to ask her to move in with us forever?" I asked with a grin.

Mom shook her head. "No, although you might be on to something . . . Lauren, her mother called me this morning. She'd gotten our name and number from Ms. Powell, and she just wanted to check on her daughter."

So far, it sounded reasonable enough.

Mom went on: "I mentioned the bike accident, and Mrs. Hollis said we must have misunderstood what Annette had told us, because Annette doesn't know how to ride a bike. I think she made up the story because she's embarrassed to tell you the truth."

"She ought to be! A fifth-grader, and she doesn't know how to ride a bike?"

"Sssh!" My mother lowered her own voice. "I have a feeling Annette doesn't know how to do a lot of outdoor things."

"She told Darlene she thought sports were stupid . . . ," I said slowly. I began to wonder, was she just covering up?

"Probably because she's never learned to play them," my mom said, echoing my thoughts. "An-

58

nette is an only child, and I get the idea her mother is one of those nervous people who worries about everything — especially when it comes to her daughter.''

I nodded, beginning to understand a little.

''Mrs. Hollis worries that Annette's going to get hurt, so she has discouraged her from riding a bike, roller-skating, playing baseball. . . . Every time I mentioned something you girls might do together this week, Mrs. Hollis sounded anxious about it.''

I tried to imagine not doing those things, but I couldn't. I knew how to catch a baseball when I was five years old — Roger had taught me.

''Besides,'' I said out loud, continuing that line of thinking, ''even if you'd told me I couldn't, I probably would have learned from my friends anyway.''

''Apparently the Hollises have moved a great deal because of Mr. Hollis's job,'' Mom said.

People who teach or work at schools seem to move a lot — Patti's parents, both professors, have moved two or three times. There was even a recent false alarm, when the Sleepover Friends thought Patti would be moving to Alaska! Remembering how miserable Patti had been then made me feel a little more sympathetic toward Annette.

"I don't think Annette has had time enough in any one place to make close friends like you and Kate and Stephanie and Patti," my mother went on.

"Maybe she just plain doesn't know how to do that, either," I said.

"Maybe," Mom agreed. "Maybe she cleaned up your room because she wants to be your friend, and neatening up is what she does best."

"Should I do something to help her, Mom?" I asked. I wasn't being entirely unselfish. I wanted Annette to loosen up so I could spend the week with the other Walden kids and my friends!

That's when the telephone rang. I grabbed it off the wall. "Hello?"

"Hi!" It was Patti. "If you're not doing anything, I thought I'd ride my bike over and keep you company for a while . . . meet Annette . . . like that?" she said softly.

Good old Patti. She realized how lonesome I was without her and Stephanie and Kate. "Great!" I said. Then I had one of my more brilliant ideas. "Listen, when you get here, would you mind pretending you don't know much about playing baseball?"

Meanwhile, Patti's one of the best players around. She can run really fast and hit like crazy. She's always one of the first chosen for a team by boys or girls.

"Sure," Patti said. "But why?"

I lowered my voice. "Because Annette doesn't know how, but she doesn't know that I know she doesn't. You and I might be able to teach her something without making her feel crummy," I explained.

"Check!" said Patti. "See you in four." Four minutes is about how long it takes her to ride from her house on Mill Road to my house on Pine Street.

"I wonder who that could be?" I said to Annette when Bullwinkle started barking from the backyard. She was dusting the books on my bookshelves. I was trying to look casual, but I shouldn't have worried: Annette was too busy watching out for charging dogs to think about a set-up.

I trotted downstairs again and opened the front door. "Why, Patti!" I squealed loud enough to be heard in the next county. "What brings you here?"

Annette walked down the upstairs hall and stood at the top of the stairs.

"Well . . . uh . . . I just happened to be passing,

and I thought you might be able to help me with this
. . . uh . . . problem that I have," Patti fumbled.
She's not very good at fibbing.

"What problem is that?" I asked her.

"I'm . . . uh . . . I'm afraid I'm going to . . . uh
. . . flunk" — Patti probably never used that word
before in her life, since she always makes straight
A's — "flunk gym, if I don't get better at baseball,"
she said. She glanced up at Annette.

"I don't think you've officially met my guest,"
I said to Patti. "Patti — Annette Hollis. Annette —
Patti Jenkins."

"Hello," Patti said with a smile. "Nice to meet
you."

Since Patti doesn't look at all threatening, Annette sounded friendly enough when she said hello
back.

"Maybe we *can* help you with your baseball,"
I said. "Is it your batting, or your catching?"

"Oh . . . everything, I guess," Patti answered
brightly.

"The gloves and bats are outside in the garage,"
I said. "Let me put Bullwinkle in the spare room,
and we can practice in the backyard." I whizzed into

the kitchen and out the back door before Annette could argue.

I pulled Bullwinkle into the house. But instead of dragging him all the way upstairs, I decided to stick him in the den. He can't mess up anything in there, because the furniture is old — just a rickety armchair, a worn-out couch, and a round coffee table that Bullwinkle teethed on when he was a puppy.

I clicked on the TV and switched to a cartoon show — Bullwinkle loves cartoons, especially when they sing. Then I joined Patti and Annette, who were already waiting in the backyard.

Patti was making small talk, and Annette seemed comfortable with her, or as comfortable as Annette could be with baseball practice looming over her.

I handed Annette a catcher's mitt and Patti a bat. "Why don't you try batting first, Patti?" I suggested. "I'll pitch, and Annette can catch."

I lined us up so that the wall of our garage was right behind Annette. That way, if she missed a ball, she wouldn't have to run all over the place for it. Then the lesson began.

"Okay, Patti — lean a little bit from the hips," I'd say. "A little bit more — that's right."

Patti got into it, too. "What about the bat?" she'd ask me. "Where should I hold it? Right here . . . or a little lower down?"

"Don't choke up on it," I'd reply. "Grab it a little bit lower." I just hoped Annette was taking some of this in.

"Ready?" I'd say. Then I'd pitch a slow one to Patti, who'd swing and miss, to give Annette a chance to catch the ball.

"Point the palm of your glove straight at me, Annette." I'd throw in an instruction or two on her catching. Then she'd kind of heave the ball back to me, and we'd start over again.

After a while, Annette actually began to catch more balls than she missed or dropped. I nodded to Patti, who tapped my next couple of pitches a few yards, so that it'd look as though she was improving.

"That's better, Patti," I told her. "Maybe you should practice fielding now. Annette, how about batting?"

Annette didn't really want to give up her glove. "Lauren, I'm not very . . . ," she began, but Patti didn't let her finish.

"Please, Annette?" she said. "I really need help with my . . ."

"Fielding," I said quickly.

"My fielding is awful," Patti agreed. She handed Annette the bat and picked up an outfielder's glove.

"Since we won't have a catcher, Annette," I said, "I'm afraid you'll have to throw the ball back to me, too." That way, she could practice batting *and* throwing.

Annette nodded uneasily.

I could tell she'd listened to at least some of my instructions to Patti, because she leaned just far enough from the hips, and she held the bat in the right place. At first, though, we had a lot of swings-and-misses.

Just as Annette was about to get totally discouraged, she connected with a pitch. There was a feeble *thunk*, and the ball rolled past me toward Patti.

"Got it . . . ," Patti said, making a show of stumbling over her own feet, and then dropping the ball.

But Annette didn't even notice. She had a big smile on her face as she took a couple of practice swings with her bat.

We'd played for about an hour and a half when my mom stuck her head around the back door. "Girls — there's someone here to see Patti."

Patti and I stared at each other. "Who?"

Then Rebecca Newman strolled out onto the back steps!

"Rebecca!" Patti said. "How did you get here?"

"Walked," said Rebecca, bending down to pick up the catcher's mitt. "Hi, Annette." She looked kind of surprised to find Annette playing baseball, but she didn't say anything.

"Hi, Rebecca," said Annette, throwing the ball up in the air and catching it.

"Rebecca, this is Lauren," Patti said, since until then we'd only seen each other from a distance.

"Hi," I said. "I can't believe Jenny let you come over here — she isn't exactly crazy about me."

"She doesn't know where I am," Rebecca said. "She and Angela were talking about which boy had looked at them today, and which one they thought was the *dreamiest*, who they were going to dance with at the party on Friday, which nail polish they'll wear, blah, blah, blah, until I thought I'd scream! So I went for a walk. I told Mrs. Carlin, but Jenny and Angela probably haven't even noticed I'm gone."

"And you ended up here?" Patti said.

"I just walked around for a while, to calm down. Then I spotted a mailbox that said 'Jenkins.' There

66

was a little boy on a skateboard in the front yard, and I remembered you'd said you have a little brother."

Patti's little brother is Horace, who's six, and an okay kid for one who's kind of a genius.

"I asked him if he knew you," Rebecca went on, "and he told me where you were — and exactly how to get here."

"How about a game of catch-up?" I asked her.

Catch-up is a baseball game you can play with just four people: a pitcher, a catcher, batter, and first baseperson, because there's only one base. When the batter makes an out, he or she moves on to play first base, the first-baseperson moves to pitcher, pitcher to catcher, and so on.

"Why not?" said Rebecca. "I'll catch."

"I'll play first base," said Annette. She sort of watched to see what Rebecca would say to that, but Rebecca just turned to pick up the catcher's mitt. Annette jogged to first base.

Patti said she'd pitch, so I grabbed a bat. But we'd hardly gotten started when we heard a shrill voice coming from inside my house.

All of us turned to peer at the back door. Suddenly it banged open. Jenny Carlin and Angela Kemp stormed through it and down the steps!

"I might have known, Lauren Hunter!" Jenny screeched at me.

"Yeah, Lauren!" Angela repeated like a parrot. "Really!"

"You might have known what?" I said to them. I wasn't sure what they were talking about.

"You're always butting into my business!" Jenny yelled. "You'd better keep away from *my* guest!"

"Listen, Jenny — " Rebecca Newman began.

She never finished the sentence, though, because Bullwinkle crashed through the back door and knocked Jenny flat on the lawn!

Jenny squealed with rage, and struggled to get up. It was impossible, of course, because she had one of Bullwinkle's big, hairy feet planted on her stomach. He gave her face a long, wet swipe with his tongue.

"Patti, help me!" I said. We both grabbed the thick fur on Bullwinkle's neck and tried to pull him off Jenny, but he had decided he was seriously in love with her. Besides, Patti and I were giggling too hard to do much good. So were Rebecca and Annette.

"Bullwinkle!" my brother, Roger, thundered

from the kitchen. He dashed outside, too, apologizing to the visitors: "Sorry. I walked into the den to catch the end of the sports news . . . didn't know he was in there. . . ." Roger got a firm grip on Bullwinkle's collar and dragged him away from Jenny.

She sat up, spluttering and wiping her mouth with the back of her hand. Jenny was just about to blast Patti and me when she got a good look at Roger. Roger is definitely cute, even if I say so myself, and he was wearing his high-school track jacket.

"Why, thank you!" Jenny warbled, scrambling to her feet and brushing herself off. "I don't think we've met. . . ."

Oh, brother! Roger is in the eleventh grade.

Right now is when Kate would raise her eyebrow practically off her forehead, I thought, missing her a lot.

The backyard was a pretty wild scene by that point: Jenny was batting her eyelashes so hard she was making a breeze. Angela was cowering behind Jenny, but peeking out at Roger over Jenny's shoulder. Poor Roger was blushing and struggling to keep back Bullwinkle, who was the only one Jenny's body language had affected so far. Rebecca had her hands on her hips (actually, one hand and one catcher's

69

mitt); Annette had bolted for a safe spot behind a tree the minute Bullwinkle showed up; and Patti looked pretty miserable, probably because she knew even she couldn't fix things this time.

Then I heard a rustling behind me. I turned to see Kate and Darlene stepping through the hedge between my house and Donald Foster's. "What's going on?" Kate demanded.

Chapter
8

All in all, things worked out pretty well that day. Actually, maybe they didn't work out so well for Rebecca Newman, because she had to go right back to Jenny's house. Mrs. Carlin was waiting at our front curb in her car, and she didn't look very pleased.

But Kate and Darlene hung around for a while. The two of them and Patti and Annette and I played a little more baseball, until it was almost time for dinner.

Just before everybody went home, Kate said, "Annette, we're planning a bike tour of Riverhurst for Wednesday after school: Darlene and I, Stephanie and Molly, Patti. . . ."

I knew Kate was going to ask Annette and me

71

to come, too, so I frowned at her and gave just the slightest shake of my head — Annette's baseball was improving, but I hadn't gotten her on a bike yet!

Kate picked up on it, and stopped short. She checked her watch: "Wow! It's almost six, and my dad'll kill us if his casserole gets cold!" Both Dr. and Mrs. Beekman are great cooks, and they're very particular about serving their food at just the right temperature. "Let's go, Darlene. See you guys tomorrow."

"Bye," Darlene said to me. "Bye, Annette."

Annette smiled at her, but as soon as Patti had left, she got very serious. "I saw you shake your head at Kate," Annette said.

"Oh. Did I?" I said as casually as I could.

Annette sighed and sank down on the back steps. "My mother called, didn't she?"

While I was still trying to think of an answer, Annette went on, "I knew it! So your mom's told you that I never had a bicycle accident, that I don't know how to even ride a bike, or do anything else, for that matter!"

"No big deal," I said. "You can learn, can't you?"

Annette shook her head, miserable. "My mother

gets hysterical every time I want to try something new. . . ."

"Your mother's not here, is she? And we're not talking about hang-gliding or parachute-jumping. Look how well you did at baseball!" I told her. "Learning to ride a bike will be a snap!"

Annette glanced at me with a lopsided grin. "All that stuff about Patti needing help in gym — you made that up, didn't you?"

"So what?" I said. Then I grinned back at her. "So what if Patti's one of the best baseball players at Riverhurst Elementary?"

"Oh, no!" Annette giggled sheepishly. "How embarrassing!"

"Patti's also one of the nicest people around, so it shouldn't be embarrassing at all," I told her. "Did you catch and hit a baseball today, or not? Riding a bike is even easier, and I'll teach you tomorrow afternoon!"

My mom drove us to school again the next morning, but I was determined that it would be the last time. We'd be biking to school on Wednesday, or my name wasn't Lauren Hunter, Woman of Mystery.

Before the bell rang, Annette and I hung out on the steps with Kate, Darlene, Patti, Stephanie, and

Molly. Stephanie and Molly had on new outfits from Just Juniors, Stephanie's in red and black, Molly's in yellow and black.

"Don't look now, Lauren, but here comes Pete Stone," Kate warned in a low voice.

"And Jim Klager, and Henry Larkin, and Reggie Bennett," Patti added.

"Where's Jenny Carlin?" Stephanie murmured. "I don't want her to miss this!"

Where *was* Jenny Carlin? And Angela, and poor Rebecca Newman? I didn't see them, or hear Jenny's screechy voice anywhere.

Jenny's mouth had obviously been flapping, though, because the first thing Pete said was, "Hey, Lauren — I understand you kidnapped somebody yesterday."

"If you mean Rebecca Newman, I guess you're right," I said.

Reggie Bennett, also known as the Hunk, smiled shyly and fiddled with his sunglasses. Aha! *Body Talks* told me that fiddling means you're not as cool and confident as you look.

"Lauren saved her from a fate worse than death," Kate was saying. "Having to listen to Jenny

Carlin for one second longer than absolutely necessary."

"Lauren's a dangerous character," Henry Larkin said, "especially on the baseball field, and so is Patti. Are you girls going to be in the game on Saturday?"

"If we don't have anything better to do," Stephanie said. She's not wild about sports, but she has a surprisingly good aim with a ball. At the school fair this year, she knocked Mr. Civello into the water at the dunking booth about twenty times. He practically begged her to leave!

After the first bell had rung, the whole group of us walked into our classroom together. Jenny Carlin was already at her desk — I thought her eyes were going to pop out of her head when she saw us all. Angela and Rebecca were already sitting down, too. I guessed Jenny and Angela had been holding Rebecca prisoner inside, making sure she wouldn't be able to talk to Patti or me.

There wasn't anything they could do to stop her at lunchtime, though. Rebecca walked straight to the table where all four of the Sleepover Friends were sitting with Annette, Darlene, and Molly. She slipped into the empty chair next to Patti.

"I think Carlin's trying to turn us to stone," Stephanie said.

Jenny had stopped dead in her tracks and swung around to scowl in our direction.

"Laser-eyes," Darlene added. She really is a science-fiction-movie freak.

Rebecca glared right back at Jenny, until Jenny lowered her eyes and stamped off to an empty table. Like I said, Rebecca was a lot tougher than she looked!

Annette, too, it was turning out. Before we'd finished eating, she brought up the bicycle lesson herself. "I don't know how to ride a bike," she announced, "and Lauren's going to teach me after school today, so if anybody has any advice. . . ."

Kate and Darlene glanced at each other. "Sure," Kate said. "We'll come over."

"So will Molly and I," Stephanie said.

"Me, too," said Patti.

Rebecca just sighed, probably thinking about all the gruesome hours with Jenny she had to get through.

The afternoon went quickly. In social studies, Carol Harrison described her family's hog farm. She told us that pigs are really intelligent animals, at least as smart as dogs. (Compared to Bullwinkle, that wasn't too impressive.) But she also said that on a farm, you have to be careful not to get too attached to them.

Jim Klager told us about the antique apples the Klagers sell. I remembered reading somewhere that for a piece of furniture to be an antique it had to be at least fifty years old. I knew people paid lots of money to buy antique tables and chairs and even toys — but fifty-year-old apples?

It turned out that Jim has trees in his orchard that grow the same apples the Pilgrims were growing back in the 1600s, not the modern stuff like Golden Delicious. So it's the *kind* of apples that are antique, not the apples themselves. Jim said the older apples have much more flavor, and people pay a lot more for them, too.

Mom picked Annette and me up when school was out at three. By three-thirty, Kate, Darlene, Stephanie, Molly, and Patti were at my house to help with the bike lesson.

When you get seven girls together, you're going to have a lot of opinions on a subject. We stocked up on Dr Peppers and Cheese Doodles and went outside to discuss the situation.

"We'll start out on the front sidewalk," I said, "and take turns running alongside to balance the bike, until Annette can do it herself."

"Uh-uh." Kate shook her head. "The front sidewalk is too short. Annette will barely have time to get going when she'll have to brake, or she'll shoot right out into the road."

Annette looked pretty nervous at the thought of rocketing out onto Pine Street.

"Aren't you going to show her how to work the gears first?" Stephanie asked.

"I don't think she needs the gears at all at this stage — it'd be too confusing," I answered. "We'll just leave it in fifth, until Annette gets the hang of it."

"Right — don't touch this little handle at all, okay?" Patti told Annette.

"The brakes — better make sure she understands about the brakes," Molly warned.

"Maybe this isn't such a good idea . . . ," Annette said anxiously, trying to take in everything everybody was saying.

"Don't worry. It's as easy as falling off a log," Stephanie said to soothe her.

Annette went white.

"Not a great choice of words," Kate murmured, her eyebrow raised.

We finally agreed that two of us would run alongside Annette's bike on Pine Street itself. "Start out toward Stephanie's," Kate suggested, "because the road slopes downhill a little, and Annette won't even have to pedal. She can just coast, and concentrate on keeping her front wheel straight."

And that's what we did. In the beginning, Kate trotted on one side of the bike and Stephanie on the other to steady Annette. We saved the faster runners, like Patti and me and Darlene, until Annette really got going.

She had good balance and she learned fast. It wasn't long before she was pedaling up and down Pine. A little wobbly, maybe, but Annette was definitely riding a bike.

"I'm doing it, Lauren!" she yelled. "I'm actually doing it!"

Annette took her eyes off the front wheel for just a second to glance sideways at me. "Annette, don't — " Patti began.

Too late. Annette ended up in the Winkles' lilac bush. Patti and I were pulling her and the bike out when a jogger appeared over the hill.

"Rebecca Newman!" Patti said.

"You escaped again!" I added.

Rebecca nodded her head and looked grim. "I'm not going back, either," she said determinedly. "I'll take a bus home first!"

Chapter
9

"You don't have to go back to Walden," Patti told Rebecca. "You can stay at my house!"

"Would it be okay with your parents?" Rebecca asked.

"For sure," Patti said. "They were as disappointed as I was when we didn't get a Walden visitor, and now we'll have one!"

"We'd better have Mom call Mrs. Carlin right away," I said, "or she'll be combing the streets for you again, Rebecca."

"She should talk to Mrs. Mead, too." Kate had joined us, along with Stephanie, Molly, and Darlene.

Annette had been standing next to her bike, but

when we started up the street toward my house, she climbed on and pedaled after us.

"Annette!" Rebecca exclaimed. "You know how to ride already!"

Annette nodded proudly, the tip of her tongue showing between her teeth as she concentrated on staying up.

When we got to my house, Patti called her folks, who said right away that Rebecca could stay with them for the rest of the week.

Mom put the eight of us in the kitchen while she called Mrs. Carlin from the upstairs phone. If we didn't talk, we could hear most of Mom's end of the conversation, anyway.

"Hello . . . Mrs. Carlin? This is Ann Hunter, Lauren's mother. . . . That's right. I just wanted to let you know that Rebecca Newman is here at our house — I didn't want you to worry. . . . Well, the girls seem to be having some sort of little difficulty. . . ."

In the kitchen, Rebecca rolled her eyes.

"No, I don't know exactly what the problem is. . . . I'm sorry to hear that. When Lauren has a headache, a nap usually helps. . . . Yes, I'll let Mrs.

82

Mead know. I hope Jenny will be feeling better soon — good-bye."

After a few moments of silence, we heard Mom talking to Mrs. Jenkins and then to Mrs. Mead, explaining the situation to them. Finally, she hung up. "Done!" she called from upstairs.

"Yay!" we all shouted in the kitchen.

"Mrs. Mead will take care of the details, but I think you girls can just relax for now," Mom told us when she came downstairs.

We polished off the Dr Pepper and Cheese Doodles to celebrate.

"What made you leave?" Stephanie asked Rebecca around a mouthful of popcorn.

"Jenny had been giving me a hard time since I came over here yesterday," Rebecca said. "Then I dared to sit with you guys at lunch today. That really did it. Two straight hours of griping, and I couldn't take anymore."

"Don't you think she's kind of sad?" Patti said thoughtfully.

"Sad? Jenny Carlin?" said Kate.

Patti nodded. "She uses up so much energy disliking people."

"And now you and Rebecca will be sharing first place with me on the Carlin Most Disliked List," I said to Patti.

Everybody giggled.

"I know what Patti means, though," Stephanie said. "If Jenny would get off everyone else's case and think about the awful impression she's making, especially on boys — "

"Hey — that's an idea!" I said. "Maybe Jenny really doesn't *know* how she looks to other people." After the way things had turned out with Annette, I was beginning to wonder if it was *all* Jenny's fault things had gotten so crummy between us. I was getting kind of tired of always fighting with her, anyway.

"So?" Kate and Stephanie said.

"So she should read *Body Talks*!" I replied.

"Oh, Lauren!" Kate rolled her eyes.

"What's *Body Talks*?" Annette asked me.

"A book I got from Stephanie's dad," I answered, making a face at Kate and Stephanie. "It's all about how your body gives away what you're thinking and feeling."

I'd already read the book through, so I didn't need *Body Talks* anymore. I was ready to move on to *Body Conversations*, like Mr. Green. But I couldn't just hand the book to Jenny — she'd think it was some kind of trick.

"You could slip it into her desk," Patti said. She had been thinking what I was thinking.

"You're right — before school tomorrow!" I said.

The next morning, Annette rode to school with Patti, Rebecca — on Patti's mom's bike — Kate, Darlene, Stephanie, and Molly the usual way, on South Road. And I zipped down Riverdale, the street that runs behind Riverhurst Elementary.

I hid my bike behind the dumpster in back of the building. Then I sneaked through the side door and into 5B with my copy of *Body Talks*, which I stuck into Jenny Carlin's desk. I raced outside and pedaled around to the bike rack just in time to meet the gang.

When Jenny got out of her mother's car and saw us all standing there, her eyes narrowed to little pinpoints of anger. She flounced past us and through the front door in a fury.

But by the time the first bell had rung and we'd hurried inside ourselves, her expression had changed.

Sitting smugly at her desk, Jenny looked as

though she had something more on her mind than how much she hated me or Patti or Rebecca Newman. I knew she'd found the book, because she had the beginnings of her cat-who-ate-forty-canaries smile on her face. She never would have guessed in a million years that I was the one who had put it there!

In social studies, Tommy Nixon and Darlene talked about their lives in Walden. Tommy's father is a vet, so Tommy told about some of the things he'd helped his father do, like deliver twin calves and sew up a deep cut on a sheepdog's leg.

Darlene's family grows fancy fruits and vegetables for restaurants and sells fresh pies in the summertime. In the winter, they run a cross-country ski business on their land.

That day after school, all eight of us biked around Riverhurst. The Sleepover Friends showed the Walden girls Tully's Fish Market, which has tanks full of live lobsters and clams and sea urchins — the closest thing we've got to Sea World. Then we circled Munn's Pond and stopped to look at the swans at the Wildlife Refuge. We stopped by to say hello to Jane and Carol, who came with us for the last leg of our tour: window-shopping on Main Street. I, for one, was starving after Darlene's talk about fresh pies, so we checked into Charlie's Soda Fountain for ice-cream and shakes.

I was sitting in a booth with Annette, Stephanie, and Molly, chugging down a banana smoothie, when Annette said, "Isn't that Jenny Carlin?"

Sure enough, Jenny and Angela were sashaying down the sidewalk on the opposite side of the street. And who was walking right behind them? Tommy Nixon and *Pete Stone*!

"Lauren, I hope you haven't created a monster," Kate said from the booth next to ours.

"Just a coincidence," I said, sounding surer than I felt.

On Thursday, Molly and Annette were the speakers during social studies. Molly's parents are both artists. They moved from Chicago to a little farm upstate. Her dad illustrates kids' books, and her mom designs clothes, which is how Molly got interested in fashion.

Then Annette told about the different places she's lived. She ended up by saying, "Riverhurst's one of the nicest towns I've ever been in," and everyone clapped.

On Friday, Rebecca and her cousin Reggie Bennett spoke to the class together, because they live on the same dairy farm, along with their grandparents, aunts, and uncles. *Body Talks* was right about people who fiddle: they *are* feeling uncomfortable. Reggie's really nice-looking, but he's definitely shy around unfamiliar people. He fiddled with the collar of his polo shirt until I thought it would rip off.

Friday was the day I realized that Kate was right, too — I *had* created a monster. Jenny Carlin had read *Body Talks*, but she had completely missed the point I was trying to make. She had twisted it to fit her personality and somehow gotten Pete Stone to follow her around like Bullwinkle in just two days!

If Pete leaned forward, Jenny leaned back. If Pete leaned back, Jenny leaned forward, like some kind of new dance. And speaking of dancing — at the party that evening, as soon as the music started, Jenny pulled Pete onto the floor and neither one of them danced with anyone else. I don't think either of them spoke to a single other person!

The theme of the party was Sock Hop. Sock hops are left over from thirty-five years ago, when high-school kids would kick off their penny-loafers and dance around in their thick, white socks. Ms. Gilberto, our art teacher, was the deejay. She played great music, and I had a perfectly good time.

Most of the time, I danced or talked with the gang. I also danced with Mark Freedman and Michael Pastore from 5A. Michael made me promise to bring everybody to play baseball the next day — the vacant lot where they have their Saturday games is next to Michael's house on Gaton Lane.

I even danced with Reggie. Rebecca got us all to ask him at least once, because he never would have danced with anyone, otherwise. He's better looking up close than he is from a distance.

Still, it really griped me that Jenny Carlin spent a lot of the hop looking over her shoulder, to be sure I noticed her boogying away in her pink tube socks with Pete!

Chapter
10

The party was over at six-thirty, and Patti's parents picked us up in their two cars. Annette and I squeezed into Mrs. Jenkins's compact, along with Kate and Darlene.

"Did you have a good time?" Mrs. Jenkins asked us after she'd been introduced to all the Walden girls.

"It was great!" Darlene said. "I danced so much my feet are about to drop off!"

"If you'd danced with Henry Larkin, your feet *would* drop off," Kate said, rubbing her toes and groaning. "He must have stepped on mine twenty times at least! I saw you with Kyle Hubbard, Annette," she went on. Kyle's a boy in 5A, a friend of Michael Pastore's.

"Yes, he was fun," Annette said. "A really good dancer. And another boy named Robert Ellwanger, who seems kind of . . ."

"Nerdy?" I finished for her.

Kate and Annette and I giggled. Even Mrs. Jenkins laughed, because she's met Robert, too.

"It's okay to say, Annette," Kate told her. "Robert's pretty famous at Riverhurst Elementary. Did he ask you to the movies?"

Annette nodded and looked surprised. "How did you know?"

"If a girl even says hello to him, he asks her to the movies," I explained. Calling up Robert on the phone has been a major part of some of our sleepover Truth or Dare games. In fact, as much as Kate likes the movies, I've heard her turn Robert down at least three times.

We piled out at the Jenkinses' house with our overnight stuff. Mrs. Jenkins led us into their big kitchen, where they'd set the table with paper plates and napkins, big bowls of chips, pasta salad, and sodas. The centerpiece was a six-foot hero sandwich from Mimi's, crammed with baloney and pepperoni and onions and provolone and peppers.

"I'm in Heaven!" I said. "Let me at it!"

The second carload of girls, plus Mr. Jenkins and Patti's little brother, Horace, trooped into the kitchen just then, and all of us dug in. The six-foot sandwich shrank quickly and so did the bowls of chips and pasta salad. We were all pretty full by the time Mrs. Jenkins brought out an ice-cream cake the size of a suitcase!

"Wow! I don't think I'm ready for that, Mrs. Jenkins," Stephanie said, puffing out her cheeks to demonstrate how much she'd already eaten.

"I'm stuffed, too," said Kate. So were the rest of us.

"We'll save it till later, Mom," Patti said. "I think we'll get settled in the attic first."

The attic stairs are behind a door facing Horace's room on the second floor. The stairs are steep, and they're low, too. Patti and I have to stoop over so we won't bang our heads when we walk up, and so did Darlene and Rebecca.

I think of the stairs as being sort of like the narrow entrance to a cave, because they lead to a big, dark space, completely empty except for a few cardboard boxes, that is the Jenkinses' attic.

It has a pointed ceiling, and criss-crossing rafters that stretch across the entire top of the house. A single light bulb dangles from a cord in the center. There are only four windows, one in each wall, and they're small and round.

Patti and her parents and Rebecca had already dragged up mattresses from Patti's room and the spare bedroom, and some air mattresses and sleeping bags from Mr. and Mrs. Jenkins's camping days.

"Whoa!" Darlene said, dumping her tote on one of the air mattresses. "It's kind of spooky up here!"

"Great place for a ghost story," said Molly.

"Want to hear one?" Rebecca asked.

"Sure," everybody said except me. I admit it: I do have a runaway imagination, and ghost stories really get it going.

"Let's turn off the light," Stephanie suggested.

That made the attic even spookier, with a thin line of moonlight shining through one of the round windows.

First Molly told a ghost story she'd heard back in Chicago, and Stephanie remembered one about a ghostly cat who always appeared just before a person died. Then it was Rebecca's turn.

"My grandmother told me this story," Rebecca said. "Her grandmother told her, and she swears it's true." Rebecca obviously had told a few ghost stories before. I prepared to be scared out of my wits.

"In the old days," she went on, "just a few miles down the road from our farm, there was a big farmhouse that had stood vacant for years, surrounded by an orchard. When my great-great-grandmother was a girl, the farm was finally bought by a young man named Jason Parker, who moved into the farmhouse with his new wife, Kathleen.

"Everything was fine for a few months. Then, one evening about dusk, Kathleen was sitting in the living room, looking out the open window at the orchard. She heard a kind of patting sound and glanced down. There, just outside on the window ledge, was a fat, white hand!"

"EEEEuuuuuu!" Stephanie squealed. We all huddled a little closer together on the mattresses.

"Kathleen thought it might be a robber trying to climb in through the window, and she screamed. The hand quickly disappeared from the ledge. Jason came running, and he searched the yard and orchard. He didn't find anything, not even a footprint.

"One night, about a week after that," Rebecca went on, "the noises started. Not loud noises, just tapping sounds on the windowpanes in the living room. The Parkers didn't see anything outside at first.

Then Kathleen saw the same, fat white hand, moving up and down, its palm pressed flat against a pane of glass!

"Kathleen shrieked" — so did we! — "and pointed, and the hand disappeared. Jason grabbed his rifle and raced outside, but there was no one in sight.

"The noises went on, that night and many others. They'd start out with soft taps at the windows, getting louder and louder and ending with an angry banging on the front door, so loud it sounded like the door might break. But when Jason would jerk the door open, and stand there with his gun in his hand, there was nobody on the other side.

"Kathleen was getting very nervous. She couldn't sleep, and she didn't want to be in the house by herself, not even in the daytime. Then one evening she was working in the kitchen, mixing up some bread dough, when she thought she heard a click.

"She stared up at the high window above the stove . . . and saw a fat, white finger stuck through a hole in the window frame! The finger was wriggling slowly back and forth, like a big . . . white . . . *worm*!"

All of us screeched, and Annette wrapped herself up in a blanket!

"Jason rushed into the kitchen and found Kathleen in a heap on the floor — she had fainted."

I was about to faint myself, from holding my breath!

"He carried her upstairs to their bedroom and put her to bed. She stayed there for several days, weak and barely moving.

"Jason took to lugging around his pistols as well as his rifle. He was furious! Who was trying to scare them away, and why? When a banging started at the back door early one evening a few days later, he jerked the door open, ready to blast the guy!

"As usual, no one was there. . . . But Jason thought he felt a pressure against his side, as though someone — or some*thing* — had squeezed between him and the doorframe!"

Molly and Darlene shrieked!

"Jason slammed the door shut, but it was too late — *whatever* it was, it was *inside the house*!"

Goosebumps were running up and down my legs, and now Patti was under Annette's blanket, too.

"The Parkers thought they heard the sound of a hand patting the walls of the living room while they were trying to sleep upstairs. Then Kathleen found a print in a dusting of flour she'd spilled in the kitchen — the print of a soft, fat hand!"

I crawled under the blanket with Patti and Annette.

"Kathleen started to have horrible dreams, dreams that she was being strangled. The Parkers made plans to move away from the old farmhouse as soon as possible. The day they were supposed to leave, though, Kathleen came down with a high fever.

"That night, Jason sat by her bed as she moaned and thrashed around — her breathing was loud and raspy. Jason was exhausted himself. He closed his eyes, and dozed for not more than a couple of minutes. Then he woke with a start . . . not because he heard something, but because he didn't hear anything!"

Rebecca lowered her voice to a whisper: "The room was absolutely still. Kathleen's breathing was no longer loud and raspy. In fact, she wasn't breathing at all! And on the pillow, right next to her head," Rebecca hissed, "was a fat . . . white . . . HAND!"

All of us screamed, even Rebecca!

Scaring ourselves to death made us hungry

again, so we tiptoed downstairs and hijacked healthy slices of the ice-cream cake. We also found a pitcher of pink lemonade and carried our dessert upstairs to the attic.

Patti brought up her kitten, Adelaide, who can do all sorts of tricks, and her radio. We stuffed ourselves, and played with Adelaide, and listened to Friday-night requests on the Riverhurst radio station, WBRM. Like, "From Tod S., to Mary Beth Y. — 'Will You Still Love Me Tomorrow?' " The four of us explained to the Walden girls that Tod Schwartz is the high-school football team's quarterback, and Mary Beth Young is his girlfriend, and they're always breaking up, so she really might *not* love him tomorrow.

Then Darlene, Molly, Rebecca, and Annette told us about the other people they knew in Walden: which teachers were the nicest, which boys the friendliest or the most conceited. It turned out there was even a girl in sixth grade named Blaine Tompkins who was as boy crazy as Jenny Carlin. Which brought us around to Jenny and Pete Stone.

"She looked really ridiculous this afternoon in those dumb pink socks," Stephanie said to make me feel better.

"Pete's the one!" Kate said, disgusted. "Following her around like a sick puppy."

But I didn't care about Jenny Carlin or Pete Stone, not one bit. We thought we were doing Jenny a favor when we gave her *Body Talks*. But the book could only tell her *how* to make an impression — not what *kind* of impression to make. And if Pete Stone was silly enough not to see through Jenny's act, they deserved each other. At least, that's what I thought until the baseball game the next day.

Chapter
11

The Walden girls had a great time at the sleepover.

"I think we should have a Walden branch of the Sleepover Friends," Annette suggested before we finally fell asleep around four o'clock. Darlene, Molly, and Rebecca agreed.

We were all pretty tired the next morning. Annette and I took a two-hour nap when we got home. Then we had a fast lunch and met the other girls to bike over to the vacant lot next to Michael Pastore's house.

There was already a big group of kids there: Michael, Mark Freeman, Austin Albers, Kyle Hubbard, Bobby Krieger, and Tommy Brown from 5C,

Martin Yates, who's Tommy's fouth-grade cousin, Larry Jackson, Jim Klager, and a bunch of other guys. Michael and Mark were team captains, and they were already choosing players.

"Hey, Lauren!" Michael called out as we leaned our bikes against the fence. "You're just in time — you're on my team!"

"Then I get Patti," Mark Freedman said.

"Stephanie," Michael said, because he's seen her throw.

"Darlene," said Mark, because Darlene *looks* like a good athlete.

After I muttered in his ear, Michael chose Annette.

"Then I guess I'll take Kate," said Mark. He knows how uninterested Kate is in sports.

"Thanks for the enthusiasm," said Kate, slipping on her glasses.

Molly went to Michael's team, and Rebecca to Mark's. Once everybody had been picked, Mark yelled, "Batter up!" His team was in the field because he'd gotten to choose first. Bobby Krieger was pitching.

Sometimes Bobby's great, and sometimes he throws all over the place — you can never tell. Anyway, he struck out Tommy Brown and Molly, but Annette actually got a hit off of him, and made it to first!

"Way to go, Annette!" all the girls screamed, even the ones on Mark's team.

Then Bobby caught a pop fly from Kyle, and our team was out, with no runs.

Michael was pitching for our side. He'd scooped up a bunt by Mark and thrown him out at first. He struck out Larry Jackson, when who should ride up but Tommy Nixon and Pete Stone!

"I got Pete!" Mark yelled — it was his turn to choose.

Pete's a better pitcher than Bobby Krieger, and that's how I ended up facing Pete Stone on the baseball field.

He scowled at me as he wound up. A thought that had hit me as I drifted off to sleep the night before popped back into my brain. Was Jenny's body language working on him now because my "negative" signals had earlier? I mean, what if I'd made Pete feel so rotten that he was happy to see *any* friendly face?

Pete threw a fast ball first. I swung, and I missed.

"Strike one!" Mark roared, just in case anyone had overlooked it.

Pete smiled wickedly and wound up. A curve ball dipped over the plate. I just ticked it with the bat.

"Stee-rike two!" thundered Mark.

I was thinking too much about Jenny Carlin and Pete Stone and *Body Talks* and not paying good attention to the ball.

Pull yourself together, Lauren, I said to myself. That's it. Be yourself. And knock it out of the park!

Pete wound up again and pitched a low, fast one. I waited . . . I swung . . . and my bat hit the ball so hard, I thought it had cracked!

The ball flew way over Pete's head, over Austin Albers in left field . . . over the back fence!

"*Home run!*" Kate and Stephanie and Patti were shrieking and jumping up and down.

I smiled sweetly at Pete Stone, who grinned back at me as I trotted toward first. Maybe Pete's not a total loss, after all. . . .

My parents took Annette and me out for Chinese food that evening. When we got back home, Annette and I looked at my old photo albums. They're kind of a history of our sleepovers, starting with Kate and me posing in our mothers' dresses, and mixing up Kool-Pops in Kate's kitchen, then the later ones of the two of us plus Stephanie, practicing dance steps, or crammed into a photo booth at the mall making faces at the camera. And then there are the latest ones, with Patti, too — the night we purple-moussed our hair, Kate's surprise birthday-party that almost didn't work out, all four of our kittens at a kitty sleep-over at Stephanie's, the big celebration when Patti came back from Alaska.

"These are great!" Annette said, closing the last album with a sigh. "You and Kate and Stephanie and Patti have such a terrific time together."

"So will you," I told her as we got ready for bed. "Now that you have your own gang back in Walden."

The next day, all eight of us had a quick lunch at Kate's house. Then everybody piled into cars to drive to Riverhurst Elementary. The scene at the school was more or less the same as it had been a week earlier, with the Walden kids and the Riverhurst kids and their parents and Mrs. Mead standing around on the front lawn. But a lot can change in a week.

Like Annette . . . when she got here, she was afraid to try anything new. When she left, she could ride a bike and play baseball . . . "Roller-skating's next," I told her.

"Right!" said Rebecca. "Reggie will teach you — he's a fantastic skater. We'll all go to the rink first thing next Saturday."

"And we'll take you guys when you come," Molly said to the four of us.

"We'll have a hayride . . . ," Darlene said.

"And we'll put you to work, milking cows and slopping hogs," Rebecca teased.

"There's the bus!" Austin Albers shouted.

Ms. Powell climbed down as soon as it had stopped. "Did you have a good time?" she called out.

"You bet!" "Fantastic!" "It was major!" the Walden kids all talked at once. Then they gave a yell: "R-I-V-E-R-H-U-R-S-T! Riverhurst! Riverhurst! Riv-er-hurrsssst!"

Only on the last "Riverhurst," the Walden girls yelled, "SLEEPOVER FRIENDS!"

#11 *Stephanie's Family Secret*

"What's all the mystery?" I asked.

"That's just it." Stephanie replied. "I don't know." She shook her head and looked worried.

Kate, Patti, and I waited for her to go on.

"My parents have always told me everything," Stephanie said slowly. "But for the last week or so, they've been whispering a lot."

"They're getting you a present," Kate insisted.

Stephanie shook her head. "You know what I think it is?" she said.

"What?" Kate, Patti, and I said together.

"Remember that old movie we saw a couple of Fridays ago — *Time of Our Lives*?" Stephanie asked.

"Sure — the one where the guy loses his job . . . ," I began, but stopped myself.

Stephanie looked straight at me. "That's it," she said softly.

WIN GIRL TALK–
A BRAND NEW TRUTH OR DARE GAME!

Enter the Great
SLEEPOVER FRIENDS
CONTEST

100 Winners!

YOU can win a copy of the BRAND NEW game–Girl Talk! Play this exciting truth or dare game (by Golden) with your friends and have your own great sleepover party! All you have to do is enter the Great Sleepover Friends Contest. Complete the coupon below and return by May 31, 1989.

Playing games is not all Kate, Lauren, Stephanie and Patti do at their great sleepover parties! Truth or Dare, scary movies, late-night boy talk–it's all a part of **Sleepover Friends!**

Rules: Entries must be postmarked by May 31, 1989. Contestants must be between the ages of 7 and 12. The winners will be picked at random from all eligible entries received. No purchase necessary. Valid only in the U.S.A. Employees of Scholastic Inc., affiliates, subsidiaries and their families not eligible. Void where prohibited. The winners will be notified by mail.

Fill in your name, age, and address below or write the information on a 3″ x 5″ piece of paper and mail to:
SLEEPOVER FRIENDS CONTEST, Scholastic Inc., Dept SLE, 730 Broadway, New York, NY 10003.

Sleepover Friends Girl Talk Contest
Where did you buy this book?

☐ Bookstore   ☐ Drug Store   ☐ Supermarket   ☐ Other _____
☐ Discount Store   ☐ Book Club   ☐ Book Fair   specify

Name _____

Birthday _____ Age _____

Street _____

City, State, Zip _____

SLE988